# Spring Also Comes

## K. Kumar Bhattacharyya

pencil

ISBN – 978-93-90463-30-5
© *Kashyap Kumar Bhattacharyya, 2021*

Published in India 2021 by

*A brand of*
One Point Six Technologies Pvt. Ltd.
123, Building J2, Shram Seva Premises,
Wadala Truck Terminal, Wadala (E)
Mumbai 400037, Maharashtra, INDIA
**E** connect@thepencilapp.com
**W** www.thepencilapp.com

*For my sisters - Lopamudra and Upasana - in remembrance of a wonderful shared childhood and youth.*

*First Published in India in 2010 by Helicon Books.*

*Author photograph by Dipti Deka at Playon Studio.*

*This edited and corrected edition first Published in India in 2021 by*

*This is a work of fiction. Names, characters, places, events and incidents are either the products of the author's imagination or used in a fictitious manner. Any resemblance to actual persons, living or dead, or actual events is purely coincidental. The opinions expressed in this book do not seek to reflect the views of the Publisher.*

*"No generation has suffered  as much    from    terrorism    and insurgency as ours."*

> *( Common talk in the Frontiers of India.)*

*"It may not be bad that some traditions are going. But don't throw away all your traditions. Not all of them are bad."*

> *( Said  to the author by an elderly well-wisher  in his youth.)*

# THE COMPLETE WORKS OF  K. KUMAR BHATTACHARYYA AT PENCIL.


NOVELS

OF ANOTHER TIME
SPRING ALSO COMES
FADING AWAY

# **Acknowledgements.**

*FIFTEEN years had passed since my first novel, Of Another Time, was published and ten since my second novel, Spring Also Comes, was published. Since then over the years many of my readers, friends and well-wishers had pointed out many mistakes – some trivial, some serious – in the print of the above two novels. Some of my more serious readers had, I remember, suggested at various times that these mistakes could easily be corrected if my novels were properly edited.*

*In the spring of 2018 as I was sending out the manuscripts of my third novel to my typists to be typed I sent out copies of my first two novels to some of my well-wishers for their advice and help in getting them properly edited. During the following months I got many interesting and helpful suggestions from my well-wishers and friends regarding editing and correcting my first two novels.  Looking back to those days a few names stand out for their  hard work and sincere effort while giving me support and helpful suggestions in  editing the novels. First I would like to thank my sister, Lopamudra; my uncle, Padip Goswami, and my friend and colleague at the High Court Bar, Rakhi Deb, for pointing out many silly mistakes in a way only they can.  Then I would also  like  to  thank  my   childhood  friend,*

*Anupam Barua, for giving me support and advice regarding the general editing,*

*K. Kumar Bhattacharyya,*
*EVA'S EDEN, Guwahati,*
*31st December, 2020.*

# CONTENTS

# Part One.

WHEN I, Ishaan, first came to New Delhi in search of a job I took rooms in a crowded but certainly not a prosperous area of south Delhi. I was young then. I had left behind my parents in my hometown. My father did not like the idea of me working in New Delhi. He tried to talk me out of the whole idea. He said that I would get lost in the crowd in such a big city and would not be able to do much. He suggested that I settle down in my hometown among people I knew instead of working among strangers in a place like New Delhi. But as I had already said, I was young then and my old father's ideas did not interest me. Like most young people I thought very highly of myself at that time. I wanted to go out to the big world and do great things. Though now, I sometimes wish I had listened to my old father. Because after all these years, things did not work out as well as I would have liked them to. I did not do  anything great  in New Delhi  in  those years. What happened to me was the same thing that generally happened to the countless boys and girls who went  out to the big cities in search  of work  every  year. You  get into some kind of meaningless job where the only thing that mattered was how much you would be paid. And then, you slogged the whole day at this meaningless job and came back at night to your empty room, which you called home. After spending another sleepless night in your so called home, you again woke up the next morning and rushed to this job and slogged again the whole day...

When I first took rooms in south Delhi, I shared them with a boy of around my age who called himself an artist. Though during the time this boy lived with me, I could not figure out what kind of an artist  he was. Whether he was a painter or a sculptor or a singer or a musician... I never saw him doing anything artistic. Most of the time he was out with his friends. And when he was in, he would usually sleep or drink. Otherwise, he was a pleasant fellow. He talked freely and laughed heartily. His name was Monsoon.

On coming to New Delhi I had gone to a friend's place to enquire about rented rooms which I needed urgently. It was at this friend's place I first met Monsoon. When Monsoon heard about my problem he offered to share his rented rooms with me. He said he lived alone and would not mind sharing his rooms with me. I liked the idea and agreed to move in with Monsoon if I was allowed to share the costs. That was how I and Monsoon started living together.

It took me a couple of months to find a regular ten to five job. Finding a regular job in New Delhi at that time was not easy as the number of jobs were few and people wanting a job were many. Monsoon did not care about jobs. He used to say that jobs are for common people. Artists like him did not need one.

The job I finally got into was in a firm which was into marketing household accessories. What they did was, they would buy up different goods like furniture, bathroom accessories, clothes at a low price from their contacts from different parts of the country. Then they would sell these goods at a profit to shops that specialized in selling these goods. When I first started doing this job I was given to understand that my work would be that of a junior executive. But the work I was generally given had very little to do with that of an executive. Most of the time it involved running around over some stupid errand or the other. Soon I began to realize that I was nothing but a glorified errand boy. And within a few months I began to detest my job and hate most of the people with whom I worked. But I did not have much option except to carry on with my job. I was already on the path of becoming a regular slog that I am today.

It was only after I got the job I began to settle down in New Delhi and notice things. The rooms I and Monsoon rented were on the first floor of an apartment building. Below us, on the ground floor, lived an old man. He worked as a clerk in some department under the central government. He was an old man with singular habits. Monsoon used to call him Anand Dada. Sometimes in the evenings, Monsoon would go to Anand Dada's place to drink.

It must have been about a month or two after I got my job in New Delhi that one evening, I had returned home from office and had found my rooms empty as Monsoon was out. I washed and changed and then decided to make myself a cup of tea. But at the kitchen I found there was no sugar. So, I came downstairs to get sugar from a nearby shop.

While coming back from the shop I was about to go up to our rooms when I saw Monsoon at Anand Dada's front door.

"I heard your footsteps and was looking out to see if it was you," Monsoon said and grinned at me.

"There was no sugar I came to get some," I explained going up to Monsoon.

"Come in," Monsoon said holding my hand and taking me into Anand Dada's front room.

That was the first time I had entered Anand Dada's rooms. Till then, I had never talked to Anand Dada though I had seen him many times from a distance. My only knowledge about him was from what Monsoon had said.

Inside Anand Dada's front room Monsoon grinned and said, "Hey Ishaan, you have been in New Delhi for such a long time now and hadn't got introduced to Anand Dada yet, what a shame. Now here, this is Anand Dada. Anand Dada – this is Ishaan, the boy I share my rooms with, you know."

Anand Dada looked up at me. He frowned in an uninterested way. Then he waved with his hand to a dusty empty chair by the dusty table on  which he and Monsoon were drinking and said, "Sit."

I sat  on the chair.

Monsoon poured me a drink.

I took the glass and began to look around. The room looked as if no one had attempted to clean it  for a long time. There were cob-webs and dust everywhere. The walls looked as if they had never been painted. The furniture and the windows appeared as if no one had ever attempted to paint or  varnish them. Some of the window panes were broken. There were things thrown around here and there on the dusty floor. Through an open door I could see what must be Anand Dada's bedroom. Worn shirts and pants were lying about on the floor and on the bed. The bed sheets were soiled and had obviously not been washed for a long time.

Anand Dada himself was not very different from his rooms. His hair was uncombed, his unshaven face was rugged and weather beaten. His clothes needed washing and ironing.

"You have been in New Delhi for a long time?" I asked with a smile trying to brighten things up.

"Yes, I have been here since the time I got here. It was about twenty or twenty-five years ago when I first came here," Anand Dada said pouring himself another drink.

"Why did you first come to New Delhi?"

"To do this faltoo job that I'm in now."

"Why faltoo! Central government jobs are some of the best  jobs in the country. They pay you pretty well and they don't make you work as much as they do in other places. The job you have is better than the job I'm in now anytime anyday. Besides, the people in your office must be pretty interesting," I said as a matter of fact.

"The people in my office – the people in my office, I'll tell you what most of the people in my office are. Most of them are thieves. The only thing they are good at is taking bribes. And of course also at misappropriating and siphoning off public money with active help from their bosses, the ministers. As for my office, nothing ever happens there, I have been there for twenty-five years now. And in this twenty-five years, I have never seen a thing happen in my office except what I've already said. And as for the central government, it isn't anything different from my office. And you boy, you listen, don't try to teach me about my office and the central government, I've seen them for twenty-five years. I know what I'm talking about!"

"Well – well, let's go to better things, your youth for instance. Twenty-five years ago before you came to New Delhi – things must have been better then. You were young and life must have been bit more colourful than it is now,"     I said trying to lighten things up.

"Youth! What's youth? I suppose for most people youth is the time for the finer things of life – to make friends, to get married and to generally have a good time. These things never happened to me when I was young. I was always like this – always alone, always poor. The only people I had to call my own were my parents. Both of them died before I was fifteen. And I was so poor then, I couldn't even give them a decent funeral. After that, I've been left completely alone to fend for myself. I did what I could. But then, I couldn't do better than what I'm now. The only difference is that when I was young I was poorer than I'm now. My parents did not leave me anything. And after their death till the time I got this job I had to do everything just to get my daily bread  and survive – labouring,  running errands     for others,     rag     picking,     stealing     and everything that didn't pay and brought trouble. That's why I always say I never had a youth. Things are better now, I  at least don't have to steal to survive. I have this job now. Considering what I was when I was young, I must consider myself quite lucky to get this faltoo job. It could have been much worse. But I'm still alone as I always was," Anand Dada stopped and poured himself another drink.

I regretted what I had just said. I did not open my mouth that evening again. I quietly finished my drink and left. This was how I had got introduced to Anand Dada.

After that, I would meet Anand Dada often while going out or coming back to my rooms. And sometimes in the evenings when I had time, I would sit down for a drink or two with him. But then a drink or two is nothing for Anand Dada. He would drink before going to office in the morning and he would drink after he came back from office in the evening. When we drank in his rooms he would invariably continue to drink after I and Monsoon had left. And when we drank in our rooms after I and Monsoon would stop drinking Anand Dada would go away to his rooms and drink there alone. Not only did he drink too much but also smoked a lot. Sometimes when Anand Dada got drunk more than usual Monsoon would say, "Anand Dada, it's not you who's drinking whisky, it's whisky which is drinking you."

Often Anand Dada would swear and argue after getting drunk. Anand Dada was not a pleasant person to know. For him, everyone else was luckier than him. And he had something against the world.

Meanwhile, the world went on – I went on doing my job, Monsoon continued going around with his friends.

After about a year, Monsoon went back to his hometown. He said his family wanted him at home to look after the family business.

After Monsoon left, I was left alone in my rooms. Monsoon was a spirited companion, he knew how to brighten things up. After he left, my dreary life became more dreary. Anand Dada was the only person I had around my rooms to talk to, everyone else was too busy to notice me. A kind of fondness began to grow between Anand Dada and me.

Some months after Monsoon left, the second floor of the apartment building in which I lived fell vacant. As this floor was directly on top of my first floor rooms it interested me. Previously, the second floor was occupied by the owners, an elderly couple. Then the husband fell ill from some age related illness. After some days their son, who lived in Bangalore, came and took his parents away to live with him. The second floor remained vacant for some months. Later, it was rented out to a singular family. The husband of this family worked as a bus conductor in Delhi Transport Corporation. The wife worked in a bank in an official capacity and appeared to be well educated and from good family. They had a little daughter between them. They called their daughter Baby. When they first came to live in our apartment building Baby had not started going to school and had just learnt to talk. Not long after coming to her new home her mother got Baby enrolled in a nearby nursery school.

As for the husband whenever he was at home, he would swear and shout at his daughter and wife. I suspect sometimes he even beat his wife. He often came home late and invariably drunk. Anand Dada hardly talked with him and never drank with him. But strange as it may seem Anand Dada took a liking to Baby and Baby also liked him.

Things went on in this way for about a couple of years or so. Then one day, Baby's father died in a hospital from alcoholism. The doctors said he died of liver cirrhosis and jaundice. No one was surprised.

When Baby's father died the only people who came calling were from the bank where Baby's mother worked and a few people from the Delhi Transport Corporation. I did not see a single relative who came calling. I remember this distinctly because it surprised me at that time.

A few weeks after Baby's father died, Baby's mother rejoined her job in the bank and Baby also started going to school. Soon everything came back to normal in our apartment building. The only difference was that Baby was a bit older now and now-a-days she could go alone to Anand Dada's place. Sometimes in the evenings I would see her going down the steps to Anand Dada's place in the ground floor.

In this way, a couple of years passed. Then one evening on the way home from office I heard that there had been a massive bomb blast in a crowded area of the main road near our locality and many people had lost their lives. On getting to my rooms I turned on the television. One or two channels were running live reports of the bomb blast. I made myself a cup of tea and settled down before the television. The police was there on the spot. Both the police and the journalists said that it was the work of terrorists. They were showing mangled bodies, burning cars and the crater that was formed in the middle of the main road at the spot where the bomb went off. Just then, I heard a knock in the front door. I turned out the television and put down my tea cup. Then I opened the front door.

It was Anand Dada.

"Did you hear about the bomb blast?" he said.

"Yes, I was watching it on T.V. just now," I said.

"Did you see Baby's mother?"

"No."

"Baby's with me. A teacher dropped her at my place a little while ago. The teacher said that Baby's mother didn't go to pick-up Baby as usual from school. The teacher knew where Baby lived. So she decided to drop Baby on her way home. When they got here I met them on the ground floor. After the teacher left, I took Baby upstairs but found Baby's mother had not got home yet and the front door was locked. So I took Baby downstairs to my rooms and asked her to wash. Then I gave her a few biscuits to eat and came here. I heard about the bomb blast on the way back from office. I got worried about Baby's mother, you know."

"Wait, let me think. I had been watching the T.V. The place in which the bomb exploded was in front of our local bus-stop at which Baby's mother generally gets down while coming back from the bank. And she generally walks home from the bus-stop, doesn't she?"

"Yes."

"What do you think we must do now?"

"Do you know the bank where she works?"

"Yes."

"Then let's go to the bank, she may still be there. Sometimes they make them work late hours in these banks."

"Let's go."

"What about Baby?"

"Let's leave her at Mrs Singh's place."

"Yes, that will do."

"You take Baby to Mrs Singh's while I get my bike out," I said.

"Aatchaa," Anand Dada said and went down.

Mrs Singh was a friendly neighbour.

I locked my rooms and came down to get my motor-cycle.

Later, when I and Anand Dada got to the bank, where Baby's mother worked, we found the bank closed. The chowkidar in the bank said that the bank had closed that day at the usual time. And that he had seen Baby's mother go out as usual with the other employees after the bank closed. When we heard what the chowkidar said, I and Anand Dada got worried and went to the blast site.

At the blast site the police was still there. We told them about Baby's mother and gave them her name and physical description. The police told us that they still cannot tell how many people died and how many got injured. They only said that the number of the dead and injured were high. They were taking the injured and the dead to a nearby hospital on ambulances. The crater at the spot where the bomb had exploded had been cordoned off by the police. Along with the police there were sniffer dogs here and there and also men from the forensic department. And of course, there were a lot of frantic and agitated people like me and Anand Dada looking for people who did not return home that evening.

Meanwhile, on one side of the main road directly opposite to the spot where the crater was formed was a row of burnt cars. Fire fighters from the fire department were spraying water with huge hoses on these burnt cars from a fire engine that was parked nearby. Smoke was still rising from these cars though the actual fire had been doused by now.

On the other side of the main road was our local bus-stop that I was telling Anand Dada about that evening. A little distance from there, two city buses belonging to the Delhi Transport Corporation were burning. Huge flames were leaping out of the burning buses. Fire fighters from two fire engines were spraying water and trying to douse the fire. Presently, one more fire engine arrived with its siren blaring and got engaged in fighting the leaping flames.

A police constable engaged in trying to control the situation told us that the two city buses were set on fire by a hostile mob that assembled immediately after the bomb blast. The constable also told us that the burnt cars on the opposite side of the road however caught fire due to the heat which the exploding bomb generated aided by burning shrapnel that originated from the exploding bomb and landed on the parked cars. Getting curious, I asked the constable what happened to the mob which set the city buses on fire. The constable told us that the police had been successful in dispersing the mob with the help of rubber bullets. Before walking off however, the constable told us that the situation was not yet entirely under control.

After the talk we had with the constable I and Anand Dada got further agitated. Though we two could not do much to be of any help to the situation, we stood around and watched the chaos that was unfolding before us. We watched the people, the police, the personnel from the fire department and everyone else involved in trying to handle the situation. Besides the smoke, there was the acrid smell of cars and tyres burning all around the place.

Later that night, we went to the hospital where the authorities had taken the injured and the dead. The emergency wards of the hospital were flooded with the injured from the bomb blast site. There were injured patients everywhere – on the beds, the floor and even the corridors of the emergency wards. The doctors and the nurses were doing what they could. We began to look around among the injured patients for Baby's mother.

In the next couple of hours, we had a good look at every injured patient from the bomb blast site in the hospital but did not find Baby's mother or anybody even remotely resembling her. Getting worried we asked a nurse if there was any other place where we can look. The nurse suggested that we should check out the dead and directed us to a large room where, for lack of space, the dead from the bomb blast site were lined up on the floor. Each body was covered with a white sheet with only the face showing. We began to check the dead bodies one by one. But, we did not find Baby's mother even among the dead.

A lot of relatives and friends of the dead were crying in the room. Among them, an old woman was shaking hysterically the body of her dead son and crying. The limbs of the boy had been blown away and his lower parts had been burnt beyond recognition. But, the face had remained intact.

The faces of some of the bodies had been burnt or blown away by the blast and could no longer be identified. Could Baby's mother be among these unidentified dead?

Meanwhile the relatives and friends of the dead and injured continued to pour into the hospital. The police and the hospital authorities had set up a special counter in the reception room of the hospital to give and receive information about the bomb blast victims. People were crowding around this counter and frantically asking for information about some victim or the other. We went and informed this counter about Baby's mother. The people behind the counter noted down in a register Baby's mother's name, a brief physical description and every other information that we could give. When the people behind the counter heard that we could not find Baby's mother among the injured or the dead, they said that, in that case either she was not injured or killed in the bomb blast or she was among the highly disfigured bodies that had remained unidentified. They also said that some of the unidentified bodies had been identified by friends and relatives from body clothes or from body marks. But, we did not know what Baby's mother was wearing while coming back from the bank that day nor did we know of any mark on her body which can help us in identifying her. So, we were in a spot. Then one of the smarter personnel behind the counter went through the data he had with him at that moment and said that among the unidentified bodies brought in till then to the hospital there was only one woman and that body had already been identified by the woman's son from the clothes she was wearing. So, the presence of Baby's mother's body among the unidentified bodies did not arise. Then the personnel went on to say that in all probability Baby's mother was not injured or killed in the bomb blast. And that the bomb blast may have only delayed her from returning home or she may have suffered from some small injury and was discharged from the hospital after first-aid. This made us hope that if what the personnel said was right, Baby's mother should be home by now as some hours had passed since we left our apartment building. So we hurried home and went upstairs to the second floor of our apartment building. But Baby's mother had not returned yet and the front door was still locked. Then we came down and talked with a few neighbours. The neighbours said they had not seen Baby's mother since morning. Our short lived hope disappeared. We went to Mrs Singh's to ask about Baby.

When we got to Mrs Singh we told her that Baby's mother remained untraced. Mrs Singh said that Baby was asleep and better stay with her for the night. We agreed with Mrs Singh and wished her good night. Then we came down from Mrs Singh's first floor flat.

The next morning both I and Anand Dada had to get back to our jobs. So it was not till evening that we got back to the hospital to enquire about Baby's mother. I will not tell here how many more enquires we made to the hospital authorities and the police that evening and in the days to come. I will also not tell how many more injured and dead we inspected and enquired about, for it was all in vain. Baby's mother remained untraced. No one could tell us what happened to her on that fateful evening after she left the bank where she worked.

As for Baby, after living for the first couple of days with Mrs Singh she started living with Anand Dada. We broke open Baby's mother's second floor flat, got Baby's and her mother's belongings out, and shifted them to Anand Dada's place. We told the owner of the second floor that since Baby would now be living with Anand Dada we would no longer be requiring the flat. The owner within a few days rented the flat out to another family.

I and Anand Dada at first expected from Baby a bit of trouble with both her parents no longer there. But strange as it may seem, Baby did not create any trouble and quietly adjusted herself to her new life. Though initially she did ask us repeatedly again and again about her mother. Anand Dada told her that her mother was lost and we were looking for her and Baby should help us in our search. Anand Dada also explained to Baby that she must be a good girl and study hard at school so that when she grows up she can search for her mother on her own. Gradually Baby in her own way understood what Anand Dada said and ceased to ask about her mother. I think the idea of growing up and searching for her mother interested her.

Baby was a quiet girl, and once she had settled down with Anand Dada she did not  fuss much over anything. In the beginning, the picture of Anand Dada and Baby living together seemed odd to my eyes. But I soon got accustomed to it. Anand Dada would always drop Baby at her school every morning before going to his office. In the afternoon, he would pick her up from school while coming back from his office.

I would sometimes watch with a smile from the window of my room Anand Dada and Baby going out together in the morning or coming back in the afternoon. Baby would look very smart in her school uniform while Anand Dada with his unwashed and wrinkled clothes looked older than he was. But within a short time things started changing in an unexpected way. Anand Dada at his age began to change.

To begin with, Anand Dada hired a part time maid to clean his rooms and wash the clothes everyday. Then after a few days, he hired a painter and got his rooms painted. Gradually over the next few months he put on new curtains on the doors and windows of his newly painted rooms, replaced his broken and dirty furniture with new ones, and  got new clothes stitched for Baby. Anand Dada's own clothes also began to look well washed and well ironed. Within a couple of months of Baby's coming,  Anand Dada's rooms started looking new, clean and orderly. Anand Dada himself started looking a lot younger as not only were his clothes now fresher and cleaner, he would also now-a-days comb his hair and shave regularly. Anand Dada also began to control his drinking and smoking. I could see that he now-a-days drank and smoked less. And suddenly after Baby's coming Anand Dada had a purpose in life. These developments at first amused me but later it began to interest me.

Meanwhile, things were happening in my life too. It was during these days that I began to date Radha Iyer. She and her family were from down south. Her family had shifted to New Delhi from Chennai some years back. Radha used to work in a corporate law firm before joining our firm. When I first joined our firm we did not have a regular legal officer. But over the years our firm began to grow. As our transactions grew we began to feel the necessity of a regular legal officer to avoid legal problems. The bosses in our firm began to look around. The first two appointments did not stick. The girl who first got the legal officer's job realized within the first couple of months that our firm was too small and there was not much prospect for her career. So she moved on to a bigger firm. The boy who succeeded her was less ambitious but the firm decided to sack him before he could complete two months. I later found out from the bosses that the poor boy was sacked because they thought he had no idea what the law in our country was. Initially, I kind of sympathized with the boy and said that less than two months was too short a time to judge somebody's abilities. And in any case, the boy was not doing too badly. My bosses did not like my idea and one or two of them gave me a look as if to say the next time they decided to sack somebody it would be me. I retreated.

The next person my bosses appointed as legal officer of our firm was Radha. She was not very different from the boy she succeeded. The only difference was that she knew how to talk. And in any case I cautioned her within a week of her joining to be extra careful. When she learnt that the man she succeeded was sacked, she took my words seriously and clung on to her job. This was how our firm finally had a regular legal officer.

Radha and I began dating about six months after she joined. We were pretty serious about each other right from the beginning. We were always together in the office. And once or twice in a week we would dine out.

Later, Radha had taken me to her home a couple of times to meet her parents. I on my part once brought her to see my rooms and introduced her to Anand Dada and Baby. I still remember that day. It was a pleasant autumn evening. It had been a holiday. Radha and I had met for tea late in the afternoon in one of those uptown restaurants where Radha often insisted on going to. As we slowly had our tea Radha wanted to see my rooms. She had wanted to see my rooms many times before but I never had the courage to take her. I knew my rooms as they were would not impress her. But that afternoon, Radha insisted more than usual. Not having much choice, I agreed. And towards the evening I took Radha to my rooms.

As I had expected, my rooms certainly did not impress Radha. You know these girls, they have a kind of genius to see things that you did not want them to see. Now that evening there were many things in my rooms that I would have preferred Radha not to see at all. To start with, my rooms had not been swept for more than a week. Then my bed had remained unmade that day as I had forgotten to make it in the morning. Radha smiled at my dirty floor and my unmade bed and asked if that was how I generally lived. Then she asked where the bathroom was. I tried to explain to her that there was nothing in the bathroom that would interest her. But she insisted and so I took her. Again, as I had expected the bathroom did  not impress Radha. In fact the condition of the bathroom shocked her.

What Radha saw in my rooms did not exactly brighten her up. And then she started doing what most girls generally did in such situations, she started telling me that I must keep my rooms clean and that I must make my bed everyday and things generally on that line...

Later, I took Radha downstairs in the hope that Baby would brighten Radha up a bit and make the atmosphere more pleasant. Below, when we entered Anand Dada's rooms we found Anand Dada and Baby in the front room. Anand Dada's rooms impressed Radha especially after what she had just seen in my rooms.

"I like your rooms. They are very clean and bright. I hope Ishaan will learn a bit from you," she smiled at Anand Dada.

After that she turned to me and said, "You see Anand Dada is maintaining his rooms so well even at this age. There's not a speck of dust anywhere. You must learn these things from Anand Dada."

I opened my mouth to explain that things were very different before Baby came, but then decided not to and kept my mouth shut. Fortunately after that, Radha turned to Baby and they started talking. As I had expected Baby did brighten up Radha and she finally began to forget the unpleasant subject of my rooms. As Radha talked with Baby I turned to Anand Dada.

"Let's go out to the veranda," Anand Dada said.

I and Anand Dada came out.

Outside in the veranda, we sat on chairs and talked.

After sometime, Anand Dada said, "Let's go out to the street."

"No, let's remain here. It's pleasant here. It's very dusty outside in the street."

"No, it's just for a few minutes. I want to smoke."

"You can smoke here."

"No, Baby may see me smoking here."

"What'll happen if Baby sees you smoking?"

"I  don't smoke or drink before Baby, you know."

"Why!"

"It's nothing, it's just that I want Baby to think well of me. She is the only person I ever had in my whole life to call my own."

"Baby doesn't know that you smoke and drink?" I asked as we got up from our chairs and started going down from the veranda into the street.

"She must have seen me smoke and drink before her mother disappeared. I don't know if she remembers. But I didn't smoke or drink before Baby after her mother disappeared. Not at least after she started staying with me," Anand Dada said lighting a cigarette outside in the street.

After Anand Dada finished his cigarette we came back to the front room of the house. When Radha saw me she got up to go. Then she said good-by to Baby and Anand Dada.

Radha and I came out of Anand Dada's rooms.

Outside in the street, I stopped a taxi.

After Radha got into the taxi and drove off, I came back to my rooms.

Over the next two three years, Baby went up in school and I also got a promotion in my job. Radha remained at my office and we continued going around together. Anand Dada looked better and smarter than ever before. He would now-a-days sometimes talk pleasantly even about his clerkship.

Then one day in the height of summer, Baby fell ill. Anand Dada took her to the doctor. The doctor said he suspected jaundice and sent Baby to a laboratory to get her blood tested and analyzed.

When after a couple of days the blood test reports came in, the doctor went through them and said his suspicion was right and Baby had jaundice. And that the jaundice was of an uncommon type and not easily curable. The doctor wrote out a prescription and said that Baby should be hospitalized the next day.

So, the next day Anand Dada put Baby into the hospital the doctor had referred to. From the day Baby was put into the hospital Anand Dada also started staying in the hospital for most part of the day. He would go to the hospital once in the morning before going to his office and then again in the evening after coming back from office. He would come back home very late after the  visiting hours ended for the night. The hospital authorities did not allow anyone who is not a patient or an employee of the hospital to stay at night after visiting hours. I suspect that was the only reason why Anand Dada returned home at night. If the hospital authorities had allowed, Anand Dada would have happily stayed at the hospital with Baby even during the night.

During the first few days of Baby's stay in the hospital things went well. The doctors said Baby was responding well to the treatment. But then complications started developing. Baby started getting weak. She also started vomiting many times a day. Her food had to be stopped completely and she was on saline most of the time. During these days I sometimes would go in the evenings with Anand Dada to see Baby. On these visits, I remember sometimes Baby did not even have the strength to recognize us. The doctors started worrying and said Baby had stopped responding to some of the medicines they were administering. The doctors at first tried by changing some of the medicines. But it did not work. So they again took Baby's blood and conducted fresh tests. Besides this they started carrying out every test and analysis that possibly could be carried out on a child of Baby's age. After the reports started coming in the doctors started getting even more worried and shifted Baby to the Intensive Care Unit of the hospital. Anand Dada took a month's leave from his job and started spending the whole day in the hospital. He would only come home for a few hours at night to sleep before going back to the hospital next morning as early as he could.

It was during these days that one evening, after coming back from my office, I was trying to get some rest in my rooms when I heard a knock in the front door. I opened the door and found Anand Dada outside. He was looking more worried than usual. I asked him to come in.

Anand Dada came in and sat on a sofa in my front room. I gave him a glass of cold water and asked: "How's Baby?"

"The doctors said she is better than before. She is now responding to the medicines they are giving and if things continue to improve in this way they can start considering taking Baby out of the I.C.U. within the next few days."

"That's good news."

"Yes...yes," Anand Dada said managing a faint smile. "But, for the treatment to continue I'll need more money."

"How much?"

"A lot."

"Can I help?"

"No, I can't take any more money from you. You have already spent a lot," Anand Dada said referring to a few hospital and medicine bills I had helped Anand Dada to pay.

"What then?"

"I don't have any more money in my pocket nor in the bank. I went to my bank today. The Manager said he can't lend me any more money against my flat."

"You once told me you are the owner of your rooms. Didn't you tell that to the Manager?"

"I did. I even showed him the ownership papers. But the Manager said he can't allow me to borrow any more against my rooms. The amount that he can allow me to lend for mortgaging my rooms had already exceeded. The manager said the rules of the bank didn't allow him to lend anymore to me."

"Did you talk with the hospital authorities about this?"

"Yes. When I told them that I'm only a clerk they reduced the outstanding bills by more than a quarter. They now say that it is practically not possible to give me any more discounts. And that what they are charging for Baby's treatment is the minimum. I.C.U. treatment is very expensive, you know."

"I see."

"There is only one option now. I'll have to sell my rooms."

"Where'll you and Baby stay if you sell your rooms?"

"I'll have to rent somebody else's rooms."

"Will you be able to sell your rooms so quickly?"

"I've found a property agent who has a client who is giving a very good price."

"I see."

"You once said Radha had something to do with the law. Will she be able to find me a lawyer who'll oversee this deal and also help me with the paper work."

"Wait, I'll just ask her," I said.

I picked up my phone and got across to Radha on her mobile phone.

After I told Radha about Anand Dada's problem she said she would do what she could. She also said, it would not be much of a problem as she had many lawyer friends. She offered to meet Anand Dada next evening after office hours.

The next  morning at office, Radha told me she had talked with a lawyer friend over phone and the friend had agreed to meet Anand Dada at a convenient  date.

So that day after office hours when Anand Dada met Radha, she told him about her lawyer friend and gave him his address and phone number.

In the next few days, Anand Dada with the help of this lawyer friend of Radha sold off his ground floor rooms through his agent at a price which both Radha and I were certainly not happy with. Both of us thought that Anand Dada could easily have got a better price if he had waited a few more days. But Anand Dada said he needed money immediately to settle Baby's outstanding hospital bills and so that Baby's treatment could be continued.

After selling off his rooms Anand Dada moved into rented rooms which his agent  found for him. Fortunately, his rented rooms were not very far from his old rooms. So I continued to meet him as often as before.

A few days after Anand Dada moved into rented rooms, Baby was discharged from the Intensive Care Unit and allotted a regular ordinary cabin. She stayed in the ordinary cabin for some days before the doctors declared her fully cured and discharged her from the hospital. After that she came home.

A couple of weeks after coming home, Baby started going to school. Home for Anand Dada and Baby were now very different from the old rooms. The rented rooms were on the first floor of an apartment building. These rooms were much smaller and humbler than the old rooms.

Of the money that Anand Dada got for selling his ground floor rooms, nothing much remained. Almost half the money went to the bank from which he had borrowed to pay Baby's initial hospital bills. Then it cost him another neat amount to get the rented rooms. And of course, there were more bills to pay at the hospital on Baby's discharge.

Things went on in this way for some months. Early next year, Anand Dada told me that later that year he was supposed to retire from his job. It must have been a month or two after this an unexpected thing happened. It all started with the coming of an old woman from Kolkata one Sunday morning to Anand Dada's. I had gone that morning to Anand Dada's place to give a little present Radha had sent for Baby.

I still remember that morning, I had just given Baby the present and was sitting along with Anand Dada in the front room on a sofa and chatting. The present was some kind of a plastic toy with a puzzle in it. Baby was standing before us with the toy and trying to work out the puzzle. Then the calling-bell rang. Anand Dada went to answer the bell. He came back with an old woman who in spite of her age had remained remarkably agile. Anand Dada asked her to sit. But instead of sitting, the old woman stared at Baby in a strange way. Then she turned to us and asked, "Isn't she Nivedita's child?"

Nivedita was the name of Baby's mother.

"Yes, she is. How did you know Nivedita?" Anand Dada said.

"I! I'm her mother. I mean Nivedita was my daughter," the old woman said as a matter of fact.

"I see. Sit down," I said.

"What's the name of the child?" The old woman asked and sat on the empty sofa Anand Dada had just vacated.

"Baby."

"What can we do for you?" Anand Dada asked suddenly becoming pale and sitting on an empty chair that was near by.

"Well, as I've already said I'm Nivedita's mother. Which also means I'm Baby's grandmother. I come to take Baby home to Kolkata. That's where I live with my son."

"This is Baby's home. You can't take Baby from here whoever you are," Anand Dada said firmly.

"But I'm her grandmother."

"That doesn't make any difference. And in any case where were you all these years? Especially when Nivedita was struggling all alone here after her husband's death! And where were you when poor Nivedita disappeared, leaving Baby here alone!"

"You see, you'll understand when I tell you that I didn't even know where Nivedita was living. For that matter, I didn't even know that her husband had died and that she had disappeared, until a few days ago."

"That's not my fault. You should know what happens to your daughter."

"Yes, you are right. We were at fault also. But then you'll understand when you hear what actually happened. I mean the circumstances as it happened were beyond our control."

"I know what actually happened. I've seen it all. There wasn't a single relative beside Nivedita when her husband died. Then when poor Nivedita disappeared there wasn't anybody except me and Ishaan to look after Baby."

"You see, you'll understand when I tell you what happened before you met Nivedita and how we lost contact with her, our only daughter. It all started when she met this man, who later on unfortunately became her husband. We were living in Pune at that time. My husband, Nivedita's father, was posted there. During those days Nivedita was doing her M.A. in a college in Pune. She was always a quiet and simple girl and had never disobeyed me or her father. Most of the time she was busy with her studies and college friends. I still wonder how she got involved with that uneducated man! In any case, when she told us that she intended to marry this man it shocked and saddened both me and my husband. We tried to change her mind. Even her brother, who was much younger than her, wasn't happy about the whole affair. In any case, to cut a long story short, after she completed her M.A. she one day ran away with this man and cut off all relations  with us. We did everything on our part to find her. We even went to the police. But all to no avail. The years passed and with the years our grief grew.   My husband never got over the shock and it shortened his life. Fortunately, by the time my husband died, my son had this job in Kolkata. After my husband's death I started living with my son in Kolkata. I and my son had almost given up all hope of ever finding out what happened to Nivedita after she went away from us. Then about a month back, my son, who works in HDFC Bank, was asked by the bank manager to explain certain details about the working of the bank to an officer, who is much senior to him in rank. Now this senior officer was a lady and had joined HDFC Bank only a few days back and so was not acquainted with the working of the bank. Before joining HDFC Bank, this lady was working here in New Delhi. But then her husband got transferred to Kolkata and so she resigned her job in New Delhi and followed her husband to Kolkata. In Kolkata, she joined HDFC Bank and was asked to report in a senior position to the branch where my son works. In any case, after my son finished explaining, the lady asked for his business card. While taking out a business card from his wallet a passport size photo of Nivedita, which my son always keeps with him in his wallet, fell out  on the table across which my son and the lady were talking. The lady picked up the photo and looked at it. Then she stopped saying what she was saying and her face turned red. She stared at the photo and asked my son whose photo was it. My son told her it was Nivedita's, his lost sister. Then the lady looked at my son's business card and said that Nivedita didn't use her husband's title but always used her maiden title. On hearing this my son naturally asked the lady if she knew Nivedita. The lady said she did and that before coming to Kolkata she used to work together with Nivedita at the same New Delhi branch of a bank. Then on my son's insistence the lady told him everything she knew about Nivedita – about Baby, about Nivedita's husband's death and finally about Nivedita's own disappearance after the bomb blast. She also said that Baby is living with you now and gave my son your address. After this, my son immediately applied for leave from his job. But it took sometime for the bank to grant the leave. So it's only now that we could come to New Delhi. Yesterday afternoon we went to your address this lady had given. But found you had shifted from there. My son asked around in the neighbourhood but nobody knew your new address. It was only after about two hours my son met a lady called Mrs Singh. This lady knew both you and Baby well and gave us your new address. So that's how we got here," the old lady finally stopped.

"Where's your son?" Anand Dada asked in a voice which was certainly not friendly.

"He has gone to the local police station to ask about Nivedita's disappearance after dropping me here. He said he'll be back within a few minutes. He asked me to wait here."

"You can't take Baby."

"But she's my grand-daughter."

"How do we know that you are not lying?"

"But why should I lie? What'll I gain by lying?"

Just then the calling-bell rang. I went to answer it.

Outside, I found a young man waiting.

"Is this Anand Dada's house?" the young man asked.

"Yes," I said curtly.

"Is my mother here?"

"Did you come from Kolkata?"

"Yes."

"Come in."

The young man came into the front room along with me.

On seeing the young man the old woman smiled.

"This is my son," she said looking at Anand Dada.

The young man nodded.

"This is Nivedita's daughter," the old woman said pointing to Baby.

"What's her name?" the young man asked.

"Baby."

"Is she going with us?"

"No!" Anand Dada said firmly.

"But why?" the old woman said.

"Baby doesn't know you. You are nobody to Baby."

"But I'm her grandmother."

"Even if you are, you can't take Baby. Baby doesn't know you."

"Let's ask Baby?"

"What?"

"If she'll go with us."

"Who are you to ask Baby that? You see, you are only claiming to be her grandmother. That doesn't prove anything.

Now anybody can come from the street and claim to be Baby's grandmother. That doesn't mean that we'll allow Baby to go with anybody and everybody who claims to be her grandmother. And I don't know whether you understand or not that this is a very serious matter. We can't allow Baby to go with anybody who we don't know," I said suddenly without thinking.

"Hoo – hoo, Ishaan is right!" Anand Dada said.

"Who are you, may I ask! What relation do you have with Baby to interfere in this matter?" the old woman shouted.

"Who is he! Who are you to ask who is he! He has always been mine and Baby's unfailing support over the years. I'll not do anything about Baby without asking him. And Baby trusts him as much as she trusts me," Anand Dada said angrily.

"Baby, you'll go with us, won't you, I'm your grandmother. Your mother was my only daughter," the old woman said getting up and coming towards Baby.

Baby did not say anything and quickly retreated into Anand Dada's arms.

"Come – come, Baby, I'm your grandmother," the old woman said.

"No – no, I won't go!" Baby said retreating further into Anand Dada's arms.

"There, you heard what Baby said, I suppose that settles it. Now you can go from here," I said.

"I won't go from here without Baby," the old woman said.

"No Maa, since Baby doesn't want to come with us, we can't do anything for now. We'll have to come prepared with proper papers. For now, let's go," the young man, who had been watching everything quietly all this time, said.

The old woman reddened after hearing what her son said and then began to sob loudly. Moments later, she abruptly got up and left along with her son.

I remained behind for the rest of the morning at Anand Dada's place to show solidarity with Anand Dada and Baby. I and Anand Dada spent the rest of the morning explaining and cautioning Baby about the old woman and her son's intentions. We also asked Baby to avoid talking to strangers both at school and on the streets.

After that, things went on as usual for about a month. Then one day in the evening after office, I had gone out with

Radha and so had returned home late. On getting home, I had my bath and after that I sat in the front room with a cup of tea. I had just taken a few sips of the tea when I heard the calling-bell ring. I opened the front door and looked out.

It was Anand Dada. He was obviously in an agitated state. He came into my front room and sat on a sofa.

"Anything wrong?" I asked.

"It's over! The only decent thing I did in my whole life is finished today!" Anand Dada said in a shivering voice.

"Why – what happened?  Did you retire today from your job?"

"No, I still have a month left to retire. It's only that... that they took away Baby today."

"Who?"

"That old lady and her son."

"That old lady, who called herself Baby's grandmother?"

"Yes."

"But the lady didn't have anything to prove what she said."

"Besides her son, a lawyer and a police officer were also with her. They showed me a lot of papers which they said proved that the lady was Baby's grandmother and so had rights to take away Baby. When I resisted, the policeman threatened to arrest me and... and the lawyer charged me for kidnapping Baby! Then... then the son forcibly caught hold of Baby! Baby, who had just returned from school, wasn't even allowed to take off her school uniform!  They dragged her  away by  force!"

"Baby must have resisted?"

"Of course Baby resisted with all her might. She screamed and cried and even bit the son's hands until blood came out. But then, she's only a child. Three fully grown men were too many for her. And if you include the old lady that makes four. And... and I'm only an old man."

"Where did they take Baby?"

"They  said  they'll  take  her  to Kolkata, where the old lady and her son live."

"Did they say anything else? I mean did the old lady and her son leave behind their names and addresses?"

"The lawyer, who tried to be very polite, gave me some papers. The old lady and her son's Kolkata address is in those papers. The lawyer also said that if I read those papers I'll understand how the old lady is Baby's guardian. And yes, the lawyer also gave me his own card. He said I can contact him if there was any problem. And... and then he had the impertinence to say that the old lady and the son had nothing against me and were in fact grateful to me for looking after Baby all these years after her mother's disappearance! And that, they were doing what they were doing only because they had no other option! And that, Baby and I can always keep in touch by writing to each other. To which the old lady agreed and had the audacity to say that they had no intention of separating me and Baby! Just imagine, the impudence of first taking Baby away from me by force and then saying they had no intention of separating me and Baby!"

"Since you have the address, you'll be able to write to Baby."

"But will they allow Baby to read my letters? And even if Baby did read my letters, will they allow her to answer my letters?"

"You write and see."

"Yes, I'll do that."

"There isn't anything else that you can do now."

"Yes," Anand Dada said and left.

The next day Anand Dada wrote to Baby at the Kolkata address of the old lady and her son that the lawyer had given him. And Baby answered back promptly. Baby's reply assured us that she was in good hands and was safe.

Meanwhile, some days after Baby was taken to Kolkata, Anand Dada retired from his job. For the first few months after his retirement Anand Dada corresponded with Baby very frequently. Sometimes in the evenings, Anand Dada would come to my place and read to me Baby's letters. At times he would stay back for a drink or two.

However, after some months the frequency of the correspondence between Anand Dada and Baby began to decrease. It was then that fate began to catch up with Anand Dada. Anand Dada was retired now and had to live on his pension only. And a clerk's pension was not much. After paying his house rent very little remained for him for his daily expenses. Then to add to this, his old habits which had disappeared with the coming of Baby, began to reappear. He began to drink and smoke heavily. His clothes and rooms again began to resemble something like what it was before Baby came. His talk also began to become despondent. And like before he began to spend his time railing at the world. Things remained in this way for many years. Though, through all these years Baby continued to write to Anand Dada whenever she could. But more than often Anand Dada would not answer Baby's letters. Sometimes, he would not even open the letters and throw them on the table where he kept all the letters from Baby. The phone was no longer an option as Anand Dada could no longer afford it. As Anand Dada continued to fall  deeper and deeper into desolation and self-destruction, watching him helplessly was a torture for me. Anand Dada was one of those few enduring friends I made in New Delhi. His fall not only saddened me but also made me think about the futility of human existence and how unjust the world was.

In spite of his desolation, in spite of his self-destructive ways, in spite of his age, Anand Dada did not die. His hard life had made his physical constitution very strong. But the years passed and things began to happen. My career began to look up. I left my job in the old firm as I got a job as a senior executive in a big company. Money was no longer a problem. My new found affluence also brought with it a lot of responsibility and challenge. But  then, that was all.

Things between Radha and me did not end well. Like two foolish children we fought over something very trifle and petty that I do not even remember now. And the tragedy was we would have been so happy together. Both our families and friends had always wanted to see us together. My mother still talks about Radha. And I, after all these years often find myself thinking about Radha. Sometimes I even hope, we will meet someday somewhere and make up and be together again ...

# Part Two.

MANY years after Baby was taken away to Kolkata, one late afternoon, I was in my company chamber when I received a visit from a young man I did not know. I still remember it was in the later part of summer, I had just got back to New Delhi after my yearly visit to my parents in my hometown. The day after I got back to New Delhi I was a bit tired and so  did not get to my company chamber until in the afternoon. I had just settled down at my desk in my chamber and a junior executive was briefing me about the day's schedule. The executive was just finishing when Vidya, the secretary attached to my chamber, walked in. I asked her to be seated and wait till the executive finished.

After the executive left, I looked at Vidya and said, "Is it something important? I'm a bit tired after yesterday's journey."

"It's nothing official. It's only a young man who wanted to see you regarding some personal matter. He says he doesn't know your residential address. Shall I ask him to come tomorrow?" Vidya said.

"No, show him in," I said.

Vidya went out.

A moment later, a young man or rather a boy was shown into my chamber. I told him to sit and asked: "You have something to tell me?"

"You must be Ishaan Da?" the boy said.

"Yes, my name is Ishaan."

"I wonder if you remember Baby, Sir. It's she who sends me."

"You come from Kolkata?"

"No, I come from Guwahati."

"But the Baby I know lives in Kolkata."

"Oh yes, Baby used to live in Kolkata before. After her grandmother's death, her uncle was transferred to Guwahati. As Baby had completed her graduation from Calcutta University, she also moved to Guwahati along with her uncle. It was in Guwahati that I met Baby. We work in the same company there."

"I see."

"Baby sent me to get your phone numbers and present address. She also told me to ask you what happened to Anand Dada. She tells me that she had not been able to contact you and Anand Dada for the last couple of years."

"Oh! When I got this new job my address and phone numbers also changed and I had forgotten to tell Baby that at that time. Later, when I tried to get her over phone, I couldn't contact her. I guess her phone number must have also changed after she left Kolkata."

"I understand. I came to New Delhi on company business. When I told Baby that I'm coming to New Delhi she asked me to find out everything I could about you and Anand Dada. She also gave me your and Anand Dada's old addresses. When I went to your old addresses in the morning, I found Anand Dada's rooms locked and no neighbour could tell me where he lives or what happened to him. At your address I found someone else living there now. A neighbour  gave me your official address but couldn't give me your residential address. That's how I got here."

"I understand. How's Baby? She's a graduate now, isn't she? And she has got a job of her own. How long has she  been working?"

"Just a few months. She joined some months after she moved to Guwahati."

"This is my card. You'll find all my addresses and phone numbers on it. Can you give me Baby's address and phone numbers?" I said and gave the boy my card.

"Oh yes, this is Baby's card," the boy said and passed me over a card.

"You are Baby's colleague in the company where she works. But you did not tell me your name."

"Abhijeet Choudhuri is my name. But you didn't tell me about Anand Dada. Baby tells me that he used to look after her after her mother's disappearance."

"Anand Dada is fine. But at the moment he's in a rehabilitation centre. The locked rooms that you went to in the morning is still his home."

"If he is fine, why is he in a rehab?"

"It's nothing serious. You know he's an old man now. And since he has nobody to look after him, so, as a precaution I decided to put him in this rehab as he was complaining of weakness lately. Don't worry, he'll be all right. Ask Baby not to worry."

"But can you tell me the name and address of the rehab?"

"The CARE Rehabilitation Centre. It's in Vasant Kunj."

"Do you have anything else that you want to be conveyed to Baby?"

"No, I'll phone her. Give her my good wishes."

"Then Sir, I take your leave," the boy said and went out of my chamber.

I called my office boy and asked him to bring me a cup of tea. Then I called Vidya and asked her to bring in the papers and correspondences that had arrived during my absence. Vidya smiled and went out.

Vidya came back almost immediately with a bag full of papers and letters. Besides that she also had three large files which she said were waiting for my immediate attention. I asked her to keep everything on my table. She did so and began to brief me on the papers.

By the time Vidya finished briefing me and left, my cup of tea had arrived.

As I sipped my cup of tea and looked over the papers on my table my mind began to wander to the conversation I just had with the boy Baby had sent. I thought about Baby. I had not seen her after she was taken away to Kolkata. I had not even talked to her on the phone for almost two years. It seemed so strange how we had completely lost touch. Then my old worry about Anand Dada came back. I had not met him for almost a month. It saddened me to think how I,  Anand Dada and Baby had lost touch with each other. It all started almost about two years back. As I have already said Baby continued to write to Anand Dada over the years even though Anand Dada rarely answered her letters. And since Anand Dada could not afford to maintain a phone the only communication that remained between Baby and Anand Dada was through my phone. Whenever Baby wanted to know how Anand Dada was she would phone me. I also on my part would phone Baby whenever I could. In this way Baby and I used to keep in touch with each other. From what I could gather over the phone, Baby's uncle and grandmother took good care of Baby. They put her into a good school and took due care about her education and general well being.

Later, when Baby was older  and started to go to college she wanted to come to New Delhi to see us. But her grandmother and uncle stopped her on the plea that she was not old enough to travel alone.

About a year after Baby started going to college, I got my present job of a senior executive. After I joined my new job I shifted my residence to a much more spacious flat in a quieter locality. With the new job all my phone numbers also changed overnight. And due to my busy schedule I somehow forgot to tell Baby about the changes for about a couple of months. When I finally did try to contact Baby over the phone I found that her number had also changed. So I failed to contact Baby over the phone. After that I wrote to Baby once or twice to her Kolkata address. But, my letters came back unopened. This was how I had lost contact with Baby.

As for Anand Dada, some months after I lost contact with Baby his drinking problem started becoming even more acute. I started looking for professional help. It was then that a friend had got me in touch with the CARE Rehabilitation Centre. I liked the facilities they provided, especially, the facilities they used for de-addiction of their alcoholic patients. So, I decided to put Anand Dada under their care at my cost in an attempt to make him give up his alcoholic habits. Of course,

Anand Dada resisted to my idea with all his energy. But I, with active help from the people of the CARE Rehabilitation Centre, one day, took him by force and got him admitted into the centre. Once in, the rules of the CARE Rehabilitation Centre would not allow him to come out of their premises until the period of treatment for de-addiction would be over. In addition to this, the patients were not allowed any alcohol except for what the treatment of de-addiction required. So that was how I got Anand Dada into the CARE Rehabilitation Centre where he still was.

That evening after I got home, I phoned Baby. Baby was excited to hear from me. She repeated what Abhijeet Choudhuri had already told me. And I repeated to her what I had already said to Abhijeet. Later, Baby said now that she had got both mine and Anand Dada's addresses and also had a job of her own she would come to New Delhi as soon as she could.

Next Sunday early in the evening, I went to see Anand Dada at the CARE Rehabilitation Centre. It was around five when I got there. When the receptionist saw me she directed me to Anand Dada's living room.

Anand Dada was sitting on a chair in his room and reading the evening papers. He grinned on seeing me. I sat on another chair beside him. He was looking better than before. He had stopped resisting the people at the centre. He was now accepting his treatment gracefully. The treatment was doing him good. The people at the centre had told me on my last visit that the de-addiction process was progressing well.

"There is some good news," I said.

"What?" Anand Dada asked.

"I've been able to contact Baby over phone. I also have her address. She no longer lives in Kolkata, she now lives in Guwahati. Her grandmother died a couple of years ago. After that her uncle was transferred to Guwahati. She's a graduate now and works in a company in Guwahati. Now that she earns she says she'll be able to come to New Delhi on her own to meet us. Her uncle won't be able to stop her now."

"When'll she come?"

"As soon as she can."

"Who told you all this?"

"A boy named Abhijeet, who works with Baby in the company, was in New Delhi last week regarding some company work. Baby asked him to meet us and give us her address and phone numbers. The boy accordingly met me at my company chamber and gave me Baby's card. He told me everything. Later in the evening I phoned and talked with Baby."

"You have Baby's phone number and address with you now?"

"Yes, you can keep her card," I said and passed over Baby's card to Anand Dada.

"Is Baby married now?"

"No. She still lives with her uncle," I said and picked up the evening papers and began turning over its pages.

Later, we talked of other things.

Afterwards when visiting hours were over while going out of the centre I met a doctor I knew in the corridor.

"Doctor, do you remember me?" I asked.

"Of course," the doctor smiled.

"How's Anand Dada doing?"

"He is doing fine. He should be able to go home within a couple of months."

"Thank you, doctor."

"Now if you do not mind, you'll have to excuse me, I've a patient to attend to," the doctor said and walked away.

I came out of the centre and walked to my parked car.

One day around noon, a couple of months after I was able to establish contact with Baby, I was in my company chamber. I had just got to my chamber a few minutes back from a meeting and was trying to  settle down  in my work when Vidya came in and said: "Sir, a young man is here. He wants to meet you. He says you've met  him before. He also says he has something personal to deliver you from someone called Baby."

"Send him in," I said.

Vidya went out.

A moment later, Abhijeet Choudhuri walked into my chamber. He had an envelope in his hand.

"Good morning, Sir," he said when he got to my table.

"Be seated young man, you've something from Baby?" I said.

"Actually Sir, I do not know where to begin," Abhijeet said and sat on a chair across my table.

"How's Baby?"

"Actually she's here, Sir."

"Here! You mean here in New Delhi! Where's she, I don't see her?"

"She has gone to the CARE Rehabilitation Centre to see Anand Dada."

"But then, she could have at least phoned me."

"Actually, both of us wanted to give you and Anand Dada a surprise."

"Surprise! Surprise about what?"

"The thing is Baby and I got married last week."

"What! And I do not even know. Baby did not even care to invite me and Anand Dada. This is not fair."

"Wait, I haven't finished explaining. Actually I and Baby were engaged from before. After Baby came to know that Anand Dada was in a rehabilitation centre she decided to do something about it. She didn't like the idea of Anand Dada spending his last days alone in a rehabilitation centre. But then there was a problem. Even if we got Anand Dada out of the rehabilitation centre where and with whom will he stay? The question of Baby's uncle allowing Anand Dada to live in his house didn't arise because he was against Baby even meeting Anand Dada. So Baby and I decided to get married as soon as we could. Then we'll have a home of our own and Anand Dada will be able to live with us. When we got married last week, we did not invite anybody except the immediate relatives and no formal reception has yet been given. Baby wanted Anand Dada to attend the reception so we fixed a date about ten days from now for the formal reception. The idea is that in these ten days we'll get Anand Dada out of the rehabilitation centre and take him to Guwahati. There, I and Baby had taken on rent a modest house in the suburbs which will be our future home. Once in Guwahati, he'll be able to live in this house and hopefully also attend the reception. After the reception, Baby and I intend to settle down in that house. It'll be our great pleasure if Anand Dada also settles down with us in our home."

"Have you talked things out with Anand Dada?"

"Baby has talked to him over the phone in the rehabilitation centre in the last couple of days. And from what Baby tells me, Anand Dada has agreed to our proposal though I on my part is yet to meet Anand Dada."

"But I'm not sure if the doctors in the rehabilitation centre will allow Anand Dada to be discharged as he is under treatment."

"Baby did talk over the phone to the doctors who are treating Anand Dada at the rehabilitation centre. The doctors said that Anand Dada's treatment is almost over. And that he is completely all right now."

"The doctors had said that to me also last week. But that doesn't necessarily mean they'll allow Anand Dada to be discharged."

"I understand but Baby is already at the rehabilitation centre trying to get Anand Dada discharged."

"I see."

"And sir, I had almost forgotten. This is your invitation card to the formal reception of our marriage," Abhijeet said and handed over the envelope in his hand to me.

"Thank you."

"Sir, I'm going to the rehabilitation centre now. It would be very kind of you if you could also come with me. It's just that Baby thought you may be of help in getting Anand Dada discharged."

"Oh yes, actually I was also thinking on those lines. Wait a minute, we'll be required to clear all the  bills at  the rehabilitation centre. Otherwise, they'll not release Anand Dada even if he is medically fit. At the moment, I don't have my cheque book with me," I said and pressed the buzzer.

The office boy came to my chamber.

"Call Vidya," I said.

The boy went out.

Vidya presently came to my chamber.

"Vidya, my cheque book's finished. Did my banker send a new cheque book?"

"Oh yes Sir, I'll get it in a moment," Vidya said and went out.

"Sir, I'm not sure if you'll be requiring your cheque book. Actually I and Baby had come prepared. You've already paid the initial bills for the treatment. And I understand Anand Dada is also paying what he can. So, I and Baby came prepared to pay the final bills at the rehabilitation centre."

"Even then, I think it's I who should pay  the bills as it was I who got Anand Dada into the rehabilitation centre."

"But Sir...," Abhijeet was saying when the door opened and Vidya came in.

"Your cheque book," she said and gave me my cheque book.

"Vidya, I'm going out on personal work. It's something very pressing and it may not be possible for me to come back to office today. So, it'll be so kind of you if you could reschedule everything till tomorrow morning."

"I'll do that except that a few executives in the marketing division were telling me a little while ago that it's absolutely necessary they should talk to you now."

"Ask them to talk to me over the phone, will you?"

"Yes, I'll do that," Vidya said and went out.

"Shall we go now?" I said looking at Abhijeet.

"Oh yes Sir," Abhijeet said.

I and Abhijeet came out of my company office.

Outside, we came down to my car.

Later, when we got to the CARE Rehabilitation Centre, we checked at the reception and found that Anand Dada had already been discharged from the centre that afternoon. And that, all his bills were paid in cheque by a young girl. The people at the reception also said that at the moment Anand Dada was packing his things and getting ready to leave the centre. The young girl, who paid his bills, was also with him. When we got to Anand Dada's living room we found him freshly shaved and dressed smartly in clean ironed clothes. He had also completed his packing and was seated on a chair in his living room. Beside him on another chair was seated a young girl whom I hardly recognized. When the girl saw me, she opened her mouth to say something when a drop of tear rolled down her cheek. The girl brushed away the drop of tear, got up, and said, "Ishaan Da, you are still the same!"

"Baby – you are a lady now!" I said.

"Oh Ishaan Da, I'm so sorry. I couldn't come before."

"It's alright, Baby. You were so small – how would you've come alone all this distance."

"What shall we do now?" Abhijeet said.

"When'll you go back to Guwahati?" I asked.

"As soon as Anand Dada is ready. We have to get back immediately as we have work at Guwahati for the reception," Abhijeet said.

"I'll have to go to my rooms to get my things, then to my owner to give him the keys and tell him that I'll not be requiring his rooms any more," Anand Dada said.

"Let's go now, Baby. You and Abhijeet must come to my home before you leave New Delhi," I said.

"Of course, we'll come," Baby said.

"Let's go," Anand Dada said and pressed the buzzer.

A little later, a boy appeared. Anand Dada asked the boy to help to carry the luggage. The boy picked up the big suit-case Anand Dada had. The rest of us each carried a little of what other luggage Anand Dada had. Then we all went down to the reception.

At the reception, I signed Anand Dada's discharge papers. After all formalities were over, we went out to my car. The boy got Anand Dada's luggage into the dicky of my car. Then Anand Dada tipped the boy generously. The boy opened the back door of my car for Anand Dada to get in. After Anand Dada was seated on the back seat the rest of us got into the car and we drove off.

On the way, we dropped Abhijeet before the offices of my travel agent to enquire about the return tickets. Later, when we got to Anand Dada's rooms, Anand Dada and Baby got down from the car. After that, I drove off to my flat.

"You are a very big man now, aren't you, Ishaan Da?" Baby said sitting down on a sofa in my flat that evening.

"I! Who told you?" I said.

"From what I see. And from what Abhijeet and Anand Dada tells me."

"Oh, Abhijeet and Anand Dada must have exaggerated things."

"I didn't, it's obvious from what I saw. Everybody in your office takes you very seriously. You must be having great responsibilities," Abhijeet said sitting down beside his wife on the sofa.

"Oh yes, I do have responsibilities. But responsibilities don't necessarily make you big. Yes, I'm doing better than before. By the way did you get the return tickets?"

"Oh yes, I got the tickets for the first flight tomorrow morning. Your agent was very helpful and prompt."

"Where are you staying tonight?"

"At Anand Dada's. As the flight takes off at seven tomorrow morning we didn't want to complicate things by staying in some other place," Baby explained.

"That's good. But you two can't go without having tea with me."

"That's very kind of you, Ishaan Da. But, we don't want to trouble you anymore. Besides, we don't want to leave Anand Dada alone for long."

"Nothing doing, you two will have evening tea with me now. And you, Baby, will have to tell me about everything you did after your grandmother and uncle took you away from us," I said and then called Haresh.

Haresh was the boy who did all my cooking, cleaning and washing in the house. He had been working for me for some years now.

When Haresh came I asked him to make tea for all of us. Then I spent the rest of the evening listening to Baby as she narrated how she spent her days after she was taken away from us to Kolkata by her grandmother and uncle.

It was very late when Baby finally finished her story with active help from Abhijeet. Later that night, by the time I got back to my flat after dropping Baby and Abhijeet at Anand Dada's place I must admit that I was a bit overwhelmed by the developments of the day.

Next morning, I woke up early and drove to Anand Dada's place. I got there a little before five. The sun had not risen yet and it was still dark. Anand Dada, Baby and Abhijeet had finished their packing and were all dressed up and ready to go when I got there. Baby and Abhijeet were checking out inside in the rooms if anything remained to be done before leaving. Anand Dada was outside in the veranda. He was dressed smartly in fresh well ironed clothes. He looked younger than he was. He smiled happily when he saw me.

"Shall we go now?" I asked.

"Yes," Anand Dada said. "Baby and Abhijeet are just getting the luggage out."

"Things are falling in place for you at last, isn't it?"

"Well I must admit, I wasn't expecting anything of this kind. I've never been on an aeroplane. Baby and Abhijeet are taking me to Guwahati on aeroplane. You have been on an aeroplane many times, haven't you? How does it feel on an aeroplane? Do you think it's dangerous? Do you think it may crash?"

"Now, why should it crash! Now-a-days aeroplanes are as safe as any other form of transport. Can't you see so many people are travelling by plane everyday. Has anything happened to them? I myself have travelled by plane so many times, has anything happened to me? Travelling by plane isn't much different from travelling by bus or train. Only thing is, it's faster."

"What kind of place is Guwahati?"

"I've never been there. But from what I've heard, it's a pleasant place. At any rate much more pleasant than New Delhi?"

"I hope so," Anand Dada said as he watched Abhijeet loading the luggage into my car below on the road.

After Abhijeet finished loading all the luggage, Baby locked Anand Dada's rooms and gave me the keys. I promised to pass on the keys to the owner of the rooms later in the day. After that, all of us went down and got into the car and we drove off towards the airport. Just then, the sun rose in the eastern sky and another day began. As I watched the gathering light a sense of infinite joy enveloped me as I realized that at last something was happening to Anand Dada. And that he would not be always alone any longer.

# *ABOUT THE AUTHOR*

**KASHYAP KUMAR BHATTACHARYYA** was born in Guwahati into an old family of the frontier state of Assam in North-East India on the 1st of July, 1973. After completing his formal education he was called to the Bar in early 2000. Since then he is practising as an Advocate. When he was growing up he saw his homeland again and again ravaged by insurgency and terrorism. In early youth he saw old friends and boys next door suddenly taking up the gun and ultimately ruining their lives. Later he saw insurgency and terrorism spreading like a cancer to other parts of the world. Gradually insurgency and terrorism went on to become the greatest human conflict to have challenged the human race since the Second World War. Later when he was older and became a Lawyer he worked for long years among misguided youths. He still works among misguided youths whenever he can. Later when he started writing, he set most of his novels in the background of insurgency and terrorism in a multicultural society. His published novels are *Of Another Time(2005)* and *Spring Also Comes(2010).* His third novel, *Fading Away,* is currently in the process of getting published.

He considers the problem of misguided youths the greatest tragedy of his generation. It still haunts him and remains his concern. Besides misguided youths and multicultural societies, he likes to write from his *'memories of childhood'* and from his *'remembrance of youth'*. He has travelled a lot in the Himalayas and have lived among the people there. He believes that the Himalayas have still remained largely unexplored and undiscovered. There is much to know about the day to day life of the people of the Himalayan region which is beginning to attract the general public only now.

9 789390 463305